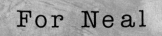

For Neal

WALTER
WAS
WORRIED

Laura Vaccaro Seeger

A NEAL PORTER BOOK
ROARING BROOK PRESS
NEW MILFORD, CONNECTICUT

Walter was

worried

when

the sky grew

dark.

Priscilla was

pUZZLEd

when

the fog rolled

in.

Shirley was

SHOCKED

when

lightning lit the

sky.

Frederick was

FRIGHTENED

when

thunder shook the

trees.

Ursula was

when

the rain came

down.

Then...

Delilah was

DELIGHTED

when

the rain turned to

snow.

Henry was

when

the sky began to

clear.

And...

Elliot was

ecsTaTic

when

the sun came

out.

Text and illustrations copyright © 2005 by Laura Vaccaro Seeger
A Neal Porter Book
Published by Roaring Brook Press
Roaring Brook Press is a division of Holtzbrinck Publishing Holdings Limited Partnership
143 West Street, New Milford, Connecticut 06776

Distributed in Canada by H. B. Fenn and Company Ltd.

Library of Congress Cataloging-in-Publication Data
Seeger, Laura Vaccaro.
Walter was worried / Laura Vaccaro Seeger.— 1st ed.
p. cm.
"A Neal Porter book."
Summary: Children's faces, depicted with letters of the alphabet,
react to the onset of a storm and its aftermath in this picture book,
accompanied by simple alliterative text.
ISBN 1-59643-068-0
[1. Storms—Fiction. 2. Emotions—Fiction. 3. Alliteration.] I. Title.
PZ7.S4514Wal 2005   [E]—dc22   2004024558

Roaring Brook Press books are available for special promotions and premiums.
For details contact: Director of Special Markets, Holtzbrinck Publishers.

First edition September 2005
Printed in China
10 9 8 7 6 5 4 3 2 1